The ACADIA FILES

Book Four, Spring Science

Katie Coppens

Illustrated by
Holly Hatam and Ana Ochoa

TILBURY HOUSE PUBLISHERS, THOMASTON, MAINE

Contents

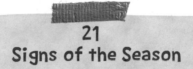
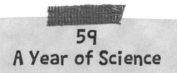
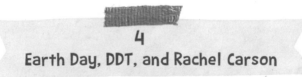

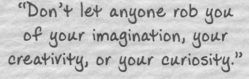

"Don't let anyone rob you
of your imagination, your
creativity, or your curiosity."
— Mae Jemison (engineer,
physician, and first African-
American woman to travel in space)

1
Catch a Falling Star

Early spring is Acadia's favorite time of year for stargazing. The air is cold but not cold enough to chase you indoors, if you dress warmly. The trees, still bare, offer glimpses of night sky through their branches. The world is quiet. *And,* when Acadia sits outside with her mom, they sip mugs of hot chocolate.

As twilight deepens toward night, more and more stars appear. Acadia likes to find constellations she's learned about, like the Little Dipper, but her favorite part of stargazing is thinking about the cosmos. She tries to imagine how big space is and how far away the stars really are. She focuses on a single star and wonders if anyone else in the world is looking at the same star in the exact same moment.

Acadia points at a bright light that darts across the sky. "A shooting star!" The light disappears quickly, and Acadia asks, "Where do they go?"

"What do you mean?" Acadia's mom asks.

"Where do stars shoot off to? I remember you telling me that the sun is a star. What will happen to us if the sun just shoots away one day?"

"It won't."

Acadia looks at her mom, who is gazing up at the stars. "How do you know that?"

"Stars don't just shoot away."

Acadia points at the sky. "Mom, we just saw one do exactly that."

"What we call shooting stars aren't actually stars. They're meteors."

"Meteors?" Acadia asks, in a tone more of protest than question. For years she has thought she was looking at shooting stars. Why didn't someone tell her the truth before now?

"Meteors are bits of rock that come into our atmosphere and burn up. What we see in the night sky is a meteor glowing with heat. Meteors can travel up to forty miles per second, and the friction generated by that speed through the air creates a lot of heat. What looks like a tail behind the meteor is actually hot gas and debris."

Acadia perks up. "So it's a space rock on fire, traveling faster than a bullet? That's awesome."

"It sure is."

"So why do we call it a shooting star?"

"A long time ago, people didn't know about meteors and were trying to make sense of what they saw, so they called them shooting stars."

"Where do space rocks come from?"

"Usually from asteroids colliding."

"What's an asteroid?"

"It's bigger than a meteor, but also made of rock. There are *a lot* of them in the asteroid belt."

"Asteroid belt? Like a belt that holds up your pants?"

Acadia's mom smiles at her. "The asteroid belt is a large band of asteroids between Mars and Jupiter. There are millions of asteroids in the band, all orbiting the sun together."

"I thought only planets went around the sun."

"Asteroids do, too. The asteroid belt separates the inner and outer planets."

Acadia looks at her mom, confused. "Inner and outer planets?"

"The inner planets are Mercury, Venus, Earth, and Mars. The outer planets are Jupiter, Saturn, Uranus, and Neptune."

"So asteroids collide and smaller pieces break off? Hmm. That's kind of like how sand and seaglass form."

Acadia's mom nods. "Exactly. The meteor that we just saw was probably smaller than a marble."

"That's tiny! Wait, you said asteroids are bigger than meteors. What if an asteroid hits Earth?"

Acadia's mom puts her arm around her daughter. "You know those dinosaurs you're so fond of? That's how most scientists think they went extinct. An asteroid that was about six miles wide hit Earth traveling . . ."

"Wait . . . . If that meteor we just saw was the size of a marble, I can't imagine what something six miles wide would do!"

"Imagine something really big, really hot, and really fast . . ."

"Hitting Earth!?!"

"The impact quickly killed plants and animals within six hundred miles. But what killed even more species was the huge cloud of dust and debris caused by the asteroid."

"Did the dinosaurs die because they couldn't breathe?"

"It was more about how the debris built up in the atmosphere and blocked the sun's rays. For months, the days were as dark as twilight. With so little sunlight, plants on land and in the water died because they couldn't get the energy they needed for photosynthesis. Then the animals that ate those plants died, and the die-off continued up through the food chain. Scientists call it a mass extinction because around 75 percent of Earth's species went extinct."

"The next time I'm having a bad day, I'm going to think about what it must have been like for those dinosaurs back then. That will remind me that things could always be worse. How long ago was that?"

"Sixty-six million years."

"Sixty-six million years! How do we know what happened that long ago? There were no people then."

"The asteroid collision explanation is a theory based on evidence."

"Are there any other theories about how dinosaurs died?"

"That's the most popular one, but some people think dinosaurs went extinct because there were so many volcanic eruptions around that time, spewing ash into the atmosphere and causing the climate to change. Other people agree that an asteroid hit but think that some of the flying dinosaurs survived and evolved over time into the birds we see today."

"Why isn't there just one answer?"

"Well, you already know about the scientific method. A scientist's job is to test a hypothesis by collecting as much evidence as she can. If the evidence supports the hypothesis, maybe it's true. But technology is always getting better, which enables us to collect more and better evidence, so what we think we know today may change tomorrow."

"Well, that's annoying," Acadia says.

"That's science! For a long time, people thought the Earth was flat and the sun revolved around Earth. As technology and our understanding improved, people changed their beliefs to be consistent with the evidence. But changing what we believe takes a long time. Sometimes a *really, really* long time. Despite all the evidence to the contrary, there are still people who think Earth is flat!"

"So when scientists provide evidence, people may not be ready to believe it," Acadia muses. "I get that. Until a minute ago, I thought I was looking at shooting stars. I had no idea they were meteors, let alone meteors the size of marbles." She leans back and stares up at the night sky. "I bet our next big discoveries will be out there."

"I think so too."

"It's weird to think about all those other planets and asteroids and things out there. It makes us seem really small."

"I find that comforting."

"Really? I think it's kind of scary."

"Earth is billions of years old. A lot has happened in our planet's history to bring us to this moment. Thinking about it doesn't scare me; it makes me appreciate life more. It makes me feel like we're part of an amazing journey." Acadia's mom reaches for her daughter's hand and gives it a gentle squeeze.

"It is kind of cool to think that where we sit right now is where dinosaurs may have roamed until 66 million years ago." Acadia moves closer to her mom, then adds, "And who would have thought that we could still be drinking their pee?"

"It always comes back to that, doesn't it?"

"Yep," Acadia says as she rests her head on her mom's shoulder and looks up at the stars.

The next day, Acadia thinks about the extinction event caused by the asteroid. She tries to picture an asteroid six miles wide compared with a meteor that's smaller than a marble. She wonders how different the impact on plants and animals might have been if the asteroid had been smaller, or if it had been even bigger than six miles. This gives Acadia an idea for an experiment.

My Impact Experiment

My First Question: Does the size and weight of a meteor impact the size of a crater?

Research: It is easier to see the impact of craters on the moon than on Earth, because the moon doesn't experience weather. There is no rain or wind on the moon to cause erosion like we have on Earth, so crater outlines don't get worn away.

Hypothesis: If a marble, a golf ball, a tennis ball, and a baseball are all dropped from the same height onto sand, the baseball will have the largest crater because it will displace the most sand.

My experimental method:
1. Get all materials.
2. Fill a container with sand (or soil or snow).
3. Spread the sand evenly.
4. Wear safety goggles to protect my eyes from flying debris.
5. Drop the marble, golf ball, tennis ball, and baseball one at a time from the same height.
6. Carefully remove "meteors".
7. Measure how wide the diameter is for each "crater".

Materials: Marble, golf ball, tennis ball, baseball, sand (or soil or snow), container, safety goggles, ruler. (I looked up the sizes of the "meteors" online.)

Data

"Meteor" diameter and weight	"Crater" diameter
Marble: 0.5 inch (1.3 cm); 0.2 ounce (5 grams)	2.0 cm
Golf ball: 1.7 inches (4.3 cm); 1.6 ounces (46 grams)	4.3 cm
Tennis ball: 2.6 inches (6.6cm); 2.0 ounces (56 grams)	4.9 cm
Baseball: 3.0 inches (7.6 cm); 5.2 ounces (149 grams)	5.8 cm

Photo of experiment:

Conclusion: The size of the "meteor" affected the diameter of the "crater". The baseball was the largest and heaviest object and produced the widest crater. The marble was the smallest and produced the smallest crater. I think this experiment would be better if each "meteor" was the same size, and the only difference was the initial speed (which would impact momentum). I'm going to retest with this question.

My Second Question: How does initial speed (and therefore momentum) impact the size of a crater?

Research: Momentum can be thought of as the force of a moving object and is measured by the object's mass multiplied by its velocity:

$$Momentum = Mass \times Velocity$$

So the heavier the object and the faster its speed, the more momentum it carries.

Hypothesis: If two golf balls of the same weight fall from the same height—with one being dropped and the other being thrown downward—the golf ball that is thrown will make a larger crater because it has more momentum.

My experimental method:
1. Get all materials.
2. Fill a container with sand (or soil or snow).
3. Spread the sand evenly.
4. Wear safety goggles to protect my eyes from flying debris.
5. Drop a golf ball, then throw a golf ball down from the same height.
6. Carefully remove the "meteors".
7. Measure the diameter and depth of each "crater".

Materials: Two golf balls, sand (or soil or snow), container, safety goggles, ruler.

Data:

"Meteor"	"Crater" diameter	"Crater" depth
Golf ball dropped	4.3 cm	1.1 cm
Golf ball thrown	4.7 cm	1.8 cm

Photo of experiment: (ball on left dropped, ball on right thrown):

Conclusion: When two golf balls of the same size and weight fall with different initial speeds, the one with more momentum will create a larger crater. The crater was both wider and deeper when the ball was dropped with a greater initial speed. Therefore, the more momentum a meteor has, the bigger its crater will be.

My cartoon of the K-T Extinction

Earth = 4,500,000,000 (4.5 billion) years old

Acadia = 0,000,000,011 years old

NEW SCIENCE WORDS

Asteroid

A space rock that orbits the sun.

Crater

A bowl-shaped dent or hole in the ground, often caused by meteorites.

Mass Extinction

When a lot of Earth's species go extinct at the same time. An example is the K-T extinction event 66 million years ago that killed the dinosaurs. A mass extinction creates opportunities for the organisms that survive. Some possible causes of mass extinctions:

Climate change: Volcanoes: Asteroid Impact:

Hot   cold

Meteor

An object from space that burns in Earth's atmosphere.

Momentum

The quantity of force of a moving object. The mass of the object multiplied by its velocity equals its momentum: $p = mv$. Momentum can be transferred from one object to another. When one billiard ball hits another, it transfers momentum. When you hit a baseball, you're transferring the momentum of the swung bat to the ball.

Meteorite

The portion of a meteor, if any, that survives the trip through Earth's atmosphere to collide with Earth's surface.

← meteorite

Things I
Still Wonder:

- What would the world be like if the asteroid that hit Earth 66 million years ago missed instead of hitting it? If the asteroid hadn't hit, would dinosaurs still be alive today? And if dinosaurs had survived, would humans be here?

- How big is space?

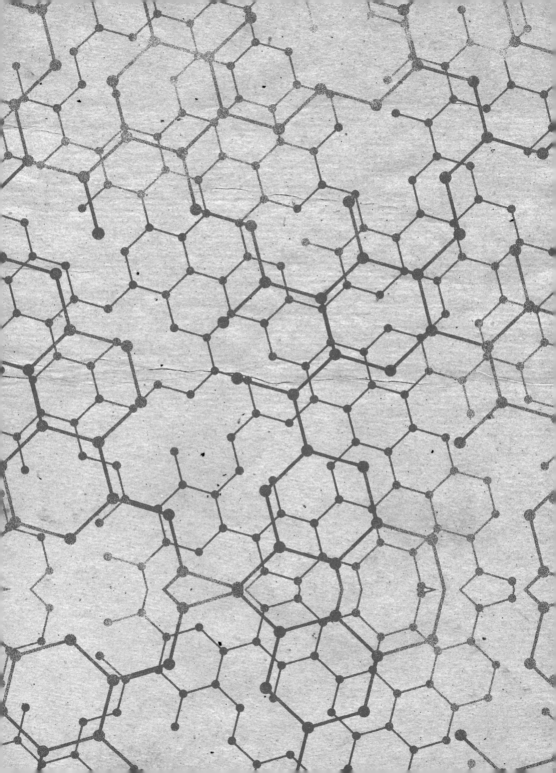

2
Signs of the Season

One early spring day, the air is so refreshingly warm that it draws everyone outside. Acadia chooses a sweatshirt instead of her puffy winter jacket, and Isabel puts on her tall green mud boots as they prepare for a walk around the neighborhood. Baxter shows his eagerness by running around in circles by the back door.

Acadia and Isabel wave to Joshua, who is dribbling a basketball up and down his driveway. He's wearing shorts and a t-shirt and seems unfazed by the patches of snow still scattered over the ground.

"Where are you going?" Joshua asks as he dribbles toward them.

"We're taking Baxter for a walk," Acadia answers. "Wanna come?"

"Sure!"

"No flip-flops to go with your shorts?" Isabel jokes.

Joshua smiles. "I can't help it. It's finally warm out!"

As they walk, Baxter investigates every puddle, and his yellow paws quickly become covered in brown mud. He pulls Acadia toward a neighbor's yard in which tufts of brownish-green grass have emerged between small piles of melting snow. Among the dull colors, Acadia notices a patch of purple flowers growing low to the ground.

"Look! The crocuses are out," Acadia says, leading the group toward the flowers.

"I don't get it. It's still kind of cold. How can flowers survive?" Joshua asks.

"How do you survive in shorts?" Isabel jokes.

"I'm tough!"

"They're tough, too," Acadia says. "They're one of the first signs of spring."

"How do they know it's time to come up?" Joshua asks. "Flowers don't have brains."

Acadia reaches down and touches one of the silky petals. "In the spring, the northern half of Earth angles more toward the sun, so we have more daylight. I'm guessing the extra sunlight and warmth give them a signal to grow."

"So the sun triggers them?" Joshua asks.

"Yep. Nature is so cool. Right now, everything that has been in a sleepy state is waking up."

"In their own way, trees wake up in the spring too," Isabel adds. "My sister is allergic to pollen, and soon she'll be sneezing like crazy."

"It's so weird to think of trees 'waking up'," Joshua says.

"Frogs are waking up too. I think I heard spring peepers last night," Acadia says.

"Is that what that chirping was? I thought someone's car alarm was going off. It was so annoying. Why are they so noisy at night?"

Acadia smiles. "Do you really want to know?"

Isabel and Joshua both nod.

"Well, animals reproduce in the spring, and to do that they need to find mates. So . . ."

"Eww," Isabel says. "You mean all those loud chirps are frogs looking for mates?"

Acadia giggles. "Yep. You can hear their call up to a half-mile away. The call helps frogs find one another. I had to learn about frogs for the letter I wrote to the town council last fall."

"That letter was amazing! Now we have trashcans by Rearis Pond," Isabel says.

Acadia smiles with pride. "Yep. It was the most important letter I've ever written. In a few weeks we can walk out by the pond and look for frog eggs in vernal pools."

"What are vernal pools?" Joshua asks.

"They're temporary pools of water that form in the fall and spring, when there is a lot of rain, but dry out over the summer. They have no fish because they're only there part of the year. That's why frogs like to lay their eggs there; without fish, their eggs and tadpoles are safer from predators."

"Thank you, Acadia," says Joshua. "That was very *rib-biting*."

Acadia groans and shakes her head. Joshua, like her dad, seems to have an unending supply of corny puns for any situation.

"Wait a minute," says Isabel. "You said animals reproduce in the spring. Do trees reproduce too?"

"That's why all that pollen will be in the air soon. That's part of how plants reproduce," Acadia says.

"I never really put it together that my sister is sneezing because she's breathing in pollen from plant reproduction. This has been a very informative—and kind of gross—walk," says Isabel.

On their way back to the house, the group searches for other signs of spring. Acadia points out where tiny buds will soon be growing on trees.

"There's your dad, Acadia. Let's go tell him what we saw," Joshua says.

Joshua tells him what he learned about crocuses and frogs and how *ribbiting* it was.

"You forgot one other way we know when it's spring," Acadia's dad says with a mischievous smile.

"When the Red Sox start playing?" Acadia asks.

"Very true," Acadia's dad says. "But there's another way too. Give up? It's when the trees look *re-leaved*."

"Wow, Dad," Acadia mumbles. "That's corny even for you."

"You really went out on a *limb* on that one," Joshua says, nudging Acadia's dad's arm.

Acadia leans toward Isabel and whispers, "Let's sneak away while we can. Once they start, it keeps going and going." The two girls skip off down the driveway.

"You know what my favorite sign of spring is?" Isabel asks.

"Please tell me you're not going to make a pun."

"Well, my *goal* was to talk about soccer."

"Really, Isabel? You too?" Acadia shakes her head. "That's all right, you're a *keeper*." Acadia grabs a soccer ball from the garage and kicks it to her friend.

Isabel kicks the ball back and says, "I think we found another sign of spring. When even you, Acadia, start making puns."

Over the next few weeks, Acadia walks around her neighborhood taking photos to document how nature makes the transition from winter to spring. Her biggest frustration is that she can't capture all the sounds and scents of spring with her camera, so she decides to make a collage of photographs and drawings, and she finds one or two photos (like the spring peeper) online. As time passes, Acadia saves space in her notebook to create a collage that includes all three months of spring, from the final snow to flowers in full bloom.

What Spring Looks Like

The first signs of spring!

Put lots of these peepers together, and they make a chorus. This little fellow is about an inch long (25 mm).

Crocuses in bloom.

Just when we thought the snow was gone, we woke up to some.

A honeybee flying to a crocus. .

Mom starting to plan out the garden.

Buds and leaves!

Daffodils.

Birds are chirping, especially outside my window!

Lots more leaves as the days go by.

Spring raindrops showing the pollen on Mom's car.

Isabel's sister sneezing from all of the pollen.

Dandelions are one of the first nectar sources of the spring, so my parents leave them for the bees instead of mowing them.

The lilacs in bloom.

The smell of lilacs in the evening air.

Iris is my dad's favorite flower.

Everywhere you look, you see green.

So many colorful flowers!

The smell of spring rain.

Clematis is my mom's favorite flower.

NEW SCIENCE WORDS

Germination

The sprouting of a plant seedling from a seed.

Hatching

A fully formed baby animal breaking out from an egg after incubation. Animals that hatch from eggs include birds, most fish and insects, many amphibians and reptiles, and even a couple of mammals (the duck-billed platypus and the echidna).

Life Cycle

The changes an organism goes through from the start of its life until its death.

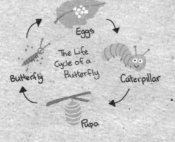

Eggs

The Life Cycle of a Butterfly

Butterfly

Caterpillar

Pupa

Pollen

Small grains produced by flowers for plant reproduction. Each grain of pollen carries the plant's male genes and is transferred from the flower that produces it to other flowers by wind, insects, or other animals. When pollen lands on the female section of a flower of the same species, it pollinates or fertilizes the flower, which then produces seeds and turns into a fruit surrounding the seeds. Seeds are baby plants; they are usually encased in a hard shell and able to survive for many years untill they find a place to germinate and grow.

Things I Still Wonder:

- I keep seeing bees near flowers. I found out that as bees eat flowers' nectar, they help the plant because pollen sticks to them. As bees travel from flower to flower, they carry pollen with them, which leads to pollination of the plants. Honeybee populations are declining, and one species of bumblebee, the rusty-patched bumblebee, has declined so much since the 1990s that it was listed as an endangered species in the US in 2017. Why are bee populations dwindling, and how can we help them?

- What would happen to plants without bees to pollinate them?

3
About Ticks

One warm spring afternoon, Acadia, Isabel, and Acadia's dad walk out to Rearis Pond in search of vernal pools. Acadia's fascination with frogs continues to grow, and she is determined to find a vernal pool that she can visit throughout the spring to observe the stages of a frog's life cycle. She looks forward to seeing squishy clusters of frog eggs, then tadpoles with their flicking tails, and then froglets, which are young frogs with a thick, long tail.

Walking through the grassy terrain, Acadia looks down at her arm and notices something.

"Um, Dad! One of my freckles is moving," Acadia says with confusion in her voice.

Isabel looks at Acadia's arm. "Wait, that *is* moving? Tick! It's not a freckle, it's a tick!"

"Movement is good. That means the tick hasn't latched on yet," Acadia's dad says, examining Acadia's arm. "It's a dog tick, not a deer tick," he says with relief as he removes the tick.

"I'm not a dog or a deer. Why was that tick on me?" Acadia asks.

"Let's get out of this grass and go over to the trail. If we stand and talk here, we could all get ticks on us."

They head to the trail and start to inspect their arms and legs for ticks.

"Here's one on my sock," Isabel says, instinctively flicking it away. "Just the thought of them makes me feel itchy. Why are they on us?"

"They're parasites," says Acadia's dad, "and parasites live on or in a host and take nourishment from them. Ticks live off the blood of other animals—like us."

"That's disgusting! They're like little vampires!" Acadia says, looking down at the spot on her arm where the tick just was.

"So, wait. If we hadn't found those ticks, they would have started sucking our blood?" Isabel asks.

Acadia's dad nods. "Most likely. They probably got onto your ankles when we were walking through that high grass. Given the chance, they'll crawl up your body looking for little nooks, like the backs of your knees, your armpits, and in your hair."

"Now I feel even itchier!" Acadia says, scratching herself. "It's like how you hear someone has lice and you can't stop scratching your head."

"Actually, ticks and lice have a lot in common," Acadia's dad responds. "They are both parasites that need a host."

"By host, do you mean that I'm the tick's dinner?" Isabel asks.

Acadia's dad smiles. "Just like we live by eating food, this is how they survive."

"So what would have happened if we didn't get those ticks off us?" Isabel asks.

"Ticks have little barbs that help them hold onto you, kind of like how a fishhook has a barb to help it lodge in a fish's mouth. Ticks will cling to the fur of a passing mouse or deer, then attach to their skin. Once they attach, they start to take in blood until they are engorged."

"I don't know what engorged means," Isabel says, "but it doesn't sound good."

"Part of the tick's body is like a tiny balloon that inflates with your blood."

"Ewww!!!!" Acadia and Isabel both say, flinching in unison.

"Baxter has had ticks on him before. When they are engorged, they look like little pale grapes with a tiny black head."

Isabel cringes. "How do you get a tick off him?"

"I get really close to his skin with tweezers and carefully pull the tick out so no part of it is left behind."

"Poor Baxter!" Acadia says.

"One of them was a deer tick, which was pretty scary."

"What's the difference between a deer tick and a dog tick? You said it was a dog tick on me."

"The most important difference between the two is that deer ticks can carry Lyme disease."

"I've heard of that disease, but I don't really get what it is. Does it have something to do with the lime fruit?" Acadia asks.

"No, nothing to do with the fruit. It's spelled L-Y-M-E, and it's a really serious bacterial disease. When deer ticks are taking in your blood, some of the bacteria they carry can be transmitted into your blood."

"That doesn't sound good. What happens if you get Lyme disease?" Acadia asks.

"One symptom is a red area that looks like a bull's-eye around the bite mark, but that doesn't always happen. Lyme disease can feel like the flu or give you really bad headaches. Your joints can get so achy that it's like you have arthritis. There is medication that helps, but we want to do everything we can to avoid ticks latching onto us."

"Yes, we want to avoid that," Acadia says. "I do not want to be a tick's dinner."

"Do a lot of people get Lyme disease?" Isabel asks nervously.

"Do you know what one of the biggest age groups is that gets the disease right now?"

Acadia thinks about how much time she spends outside and how she has always been told to do tick checks but has never really done a good job checking. "It's our age, isn't it?" Acadia says.

"Sadly, it is. One of the highest rates of Lyme disease in Maine is kids between the ages of five and fourteen years old."

"What do we do? I don't want to stop exploring the woods," Acadia says.

"And I don't want you to stop exploring," Acadia's dad says. "What are some things you can do that might prevent ticks from biting you?"

Acadia pictures how she keeps black flies and mosquitoes away when she goes on hikes. "Would bug spray help?"

Acadia's dad nods. "Yes, there's bug spray for your skin and there are sprays that go on your clothes."

"I found that tick on my sock. Maybe next time we should wear mud boots or higher socks," Isabel offers.

"That's a great idea. You can also look supercool, like this," Acadia's dad says as he pulls his socks high up over his pantlegs.

"I think that option is only for people your age, Dad."

"I'd rather look silly than be a tick's dinner," Isabel says, tucking her pants into her socks. "When we get back to your house, we could change our clothes, too. Just in case there are any ticks hiding."

"Of all the creatures in Maine, I think ticks might be the scariest, which is crazy because they're so small," Acadia says.

"Can you get Lyme disease as soon as a deer tick bites you?" Isabel asks.

Acadia's dad says, "Please hear me. I don't want you to be scared, just cautious. Not all deer ticks carry Lyme disease, and even when one does, it has to be attached to you for twenty-four hours before the disease is transmitted. If you protect yourself and do tick checks every day, you should be fine. I've been in nature a lot in my life and have found many ticks on me over the years, but . . ."

"Now we understand why you are the way you are!" Acadia says with a smile.

"Umm ... please notice that I've gone this whole walk without making a single pun," Acadia's dad points out.

Acadia raises her eyebrows and says, "Well, then you're not a very good *host* are you, Dad?"

Acadia's dad laughs, Isabel groans, and the three of them continue their search for a vernal pool.

Acadia keeps thinking about ticks and Lyme disease. She finds photos of deer ticks online and adds them to her notebook. Then she wonders whether the number of cases in Maine is increasing or decreasing. She goes to Maine's Center for Disease Control's website and makes a graph of the reported cases over fifteen years.

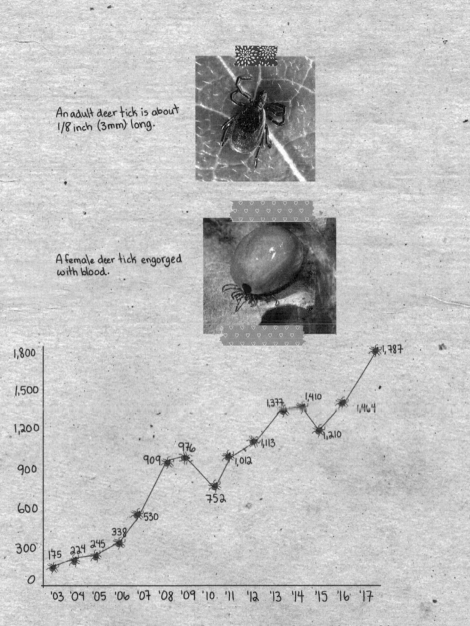

An adult deer tick is about 1/8 inch (3mm) long.

A female deer tick engorged with blood.

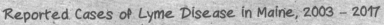

175 224 245 338 530 909 976 752 1,012 1,113 1,377 1,410 1,210 1,464 1,787

'03 '04 '05 '06 '07 '08 '09 '10 '11 '12 '13 '14 '15 '16 '17

Reported Cases of Lyme Disease in Maine, 2003 – 2017

NEW SCIENCE WORDS

Arachnids

Ticks and spiders are arachnids, <u>not</u> insects. Arachnids have eight legs (instead of six like an insect), a head, an abdomen, no antennae, and no wings.

Host

An organism that provides nutrients for a parasite.

Parasite

An organism that lives in or on another organism (its host). It survives by taking nutrients from its host.

vector

An organism that transmits a disease (or parasite) to another organism, often by biting it. The deer tick is a vector for Lyme disease.

Lyme disease is caused by spirochaete bacteria carried by deer ticks.

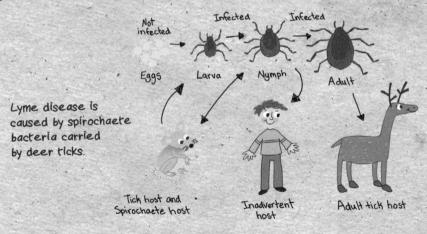

Not infected — Eggs

Infected — Larva

Infected — Nymph

Adult

Tick host and Spirochaete host

Inadvertent host

Adult tick host

Things I Still Wonder:

- Why do the rates of Lyme disease keep going up?

- Dad said you take antibiotics if you get Lyme disease. I took antibiotics when I had an ear infection. How do they work?

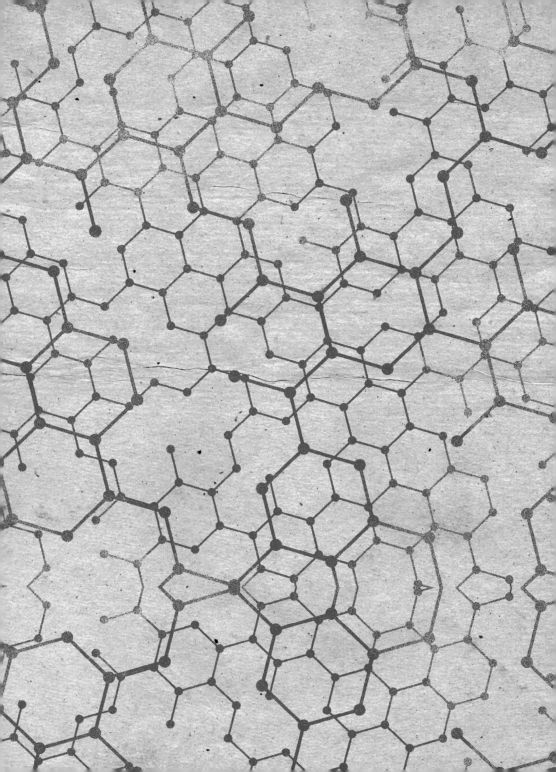

4
Earth Day, DDT, and Rachel Carson

Acadia heads downstairs wearing one of her favorite t-shirts. On it is a picture of hands holding up the planet Earth, and above that is the message *Every day is Earth Day*. "I wear this shirt all the time," she says to her mom, who is reading on the couch, "but I especially love wearing it today."

"Earth Day is one of my favorite holidays, too," Acadia's mom says, "because . . ."

"Because everyone can celebrate it. I've heard you say that just a few times."

Acadia's mom smiles. "Well, it's true. Earth is everyone's home."

"Yes, it is," Acadia agrees. She pictures what Earth may have looked like when forming over four billion years ago, what it looked like 66 million years ago when dinosaurs roamed, and what it looks like today. "Earth may be everyone's home," she adds, "but it's a home that changes in some ways but not others."

"What do you mean?" Acadia's mom asks.

"I keep thinking that dinosaurs and frogs have a lot in common."

Acadia's mom smiles with curiosity and motions for Acadia to sit next to her. "In what way?"

"Dinosaurs went extinct because of everything that happened to their environment from that big asteroid. And today, frogs are environmental indicators. Say pollution gets really bad somewhere and all the frogs die. Frogs eat insects, so if there are no frogs, there would probably be too many insects. Then, there are the creatures that eat frogs. Without frogs they'd have to eat something else. Then that could have its own effect on the food chain."

"That's an interesting comparison, Acadia."

"Sometimes nature causes the change, and sometimes people do. But one change can impact everything."

Acadia's mom puts her arm around her daughter and kisses the top of her head. "You pretty much just figured out the entire environmental movement on your own."

Acadia furrows her eyebrows and says, "What do you mean?"

"The environmental movement is about making decisions that help protect the balance of nature. One of my favorite quotes is by Rachel Carson. She said, 'In nature, nothing exists alone.' You just figured out that everything is interconnected."

"Who's Rachel Carson?" Acadia asks.

"Rachel Carson was a scientist and a writer." Acadia's mom walks over to the living room bookshelf and pulls out an old book with a light-green cover. "She lived part of her life in Maine, and she wrote this very famous book called *Silent Spring.* It changed the way we understand the balance of nature."

"That's a silly title. Spring isn't silent."

"That's the whole point. There was a pesticide . . ."

"Aren't pesticides like bug spray for plants?" Acadia interjects.

"Pretty much, yes. Her book was about a pesticide called DDT that was sprayed all over the world starting in the 1940s. Farmers used it to stop insects from eating their crops, and it was sprayed to prevent some diseases that come from insects."

"But people still use pesticides today. What made DDT so bad?"

"DDT was sprayed everywhere. Planes would fly overhead and drop it on fields below, and it was even sprayed in town neighborhoods by trucks that put it into the air like a fog."

"All that spraying must have killed a lot of insects," Acadia says. She pictures how a food web would be impacted by insects being poisoned. "But what happened to all the animals that eat insects?"

"Think about the title, *Silent Spring.* Remember learning about food webs in school? The DDT toxins don't stop with insects; they work their way through a food chain. And they stay in the environment for a long time."

"That means the chemicals from DDT could get into the soil," Acadia says. "Lots of bugs and worms live in the soil. And if the chemicals are in the soil, they can get into the crops that farmers are growing. Who would want to eat something with chemicals that are strong enough to kill bugs? Yuck!" She pictures the journey of the chemicals and what she knows about the water cycle. "Or rain could wash the chemicals into streams and rivers." Acadia creates a food web in her mind. "And the chemicals keep getting passed along as insects are eaten by fish and birds."

"Exactly," says Acadia's mom. "And DDT becomes more concentrated as it goes through a food chain. Creatures eat other creatures with DDT, and it builds up in their bodies. Some birds wound up with really high levels of DDT, which impacted their ability to reproduce. When DDT was being sprayed, bird populations went down drastically."

"And no birds means a silent spring. I get it. That *is* a good title."

"Her book helped people see the effect that humans could have on the environment."

Acadia thinks about all the different animals that were impacted by this pesticide, but then she thinks about Lyme disease and the tick checks she has started to do each day. "I get it though, Mom, why people sprayed DDT. It probably did prevent diseases from insects. I bet if we sprayed pesticides for deer ticks there would be fewer people getting Lyme disease. But it would also have a negative impact on the environment."

"And that, my darling, is the heart of it all. Just like nature has a balance, it's important to look at both sides of an issue. There are deadly diseases today, like malaria, that cause people to ask those kinds of questions."

"What's malaria?"

"Malaria is a disease that comes from a parasite that mosquitoes carry. The parasite is transmitted to people in mosquito bites . . ."

"So mosquitoes are vectors for malaria, just as ticks are vectors for Lyme disease?"

"Yes, they are. More than 200 million people get malaria each year, and around a half-million of them die."

"That's horrible."

"It *is* horrible."

Acadia looks down at her shirt. "How do we balance helping people with helping nature?"

Her mom touches the book's cover. "People wrestle with that question every day. Rachel Carson taught us to see that everything is connected. She helped us understand unintended consequences and learn to make mindful decisions about how we treat the environment. And we also need to make mindful decisions about how to help people in need."

Acadia's brain feels flooded with facts and feelings. "Can I read a little bit of this book?"

"It's very brave to try to create change. If you think about the letter you wrote to the town about the pollution at Rearis Pond, you and Rachel Carson have something in common. You both showed . . ."

"In nature nothing exists alone?" Acadia offers.

"Yes, that's true, but I was going to say that you both showed the power of writing."

Acadia looks down at *Silent Spring* and feels proud, knowing that her words helped make a difference to a little pond in Maine.

Acadia begins to wonder what else she can do each day to make an even bigger difference. She begins to research the major events of Rachel Carson's life and the history of DDT and the environmental movement. Then she draws a timeline of what she has learned. She keeps thinking about how this is *our* planet, and we are its stewards. She thinks about people in Africa dealing with malaria and comes up with some ideas to help.

A Rachel Carson Timeline

- **1929**: Rachel Carson graduates from college with a degree in biology. Born in western Pennsylvania, she visits the seashore for the first time in college. She can't swim and does not like boats, but she will become a scientist and poet of the sea.

- **1932**: Rachel earns a masters degree in zoology.

  - **1936**: She is hired as an aquatic biologist by the US Bureau of Fisheries.

  - **1937**: Rachel's essay "Undersea" appears in The Atlantic magazine. She writes of "the lilt of the long, slow swells of mid-ocean" and the lobster that "feels his way with nimble wariness through the perpetual twilight."

- **1940s**: DDT is developed to combat crop-eating insects and help fight insect-caused diseases like malaria.

- **1941**: Rachel's first book, Under the Sea-Wind, is published.

- **1945**: DDT becomes available for sale in the US.

- **1951**: Rachel publishes The Sea Around Us, in which she writes that "fishes and plankton, whales and squids, birds and sea turtles, are all linked by unbreakable ties to certain kinds of water.

- **1952**: The Sea Around Us wins the National Book Award for Nonfiction and is on the New York Times bestseller list for 86 weeks.

  - **1952**: Rachel Carson quits her government job and becomes a full-time writer.

  - **1955**: Rachel's book The Edge of the Sea becomes another bestseller.

- **1958**: Olga Owens Huckins, a Massachusetts birdwatcher, writes a letter to Rachel describing how she found dead birds the day after DDT was sprayed. Rachel begins to research the impacts of DDT on the environment.

- 1960: Rachel is diagnosed with breast cancer.

- 1962: Rachel's book <u>Silent Spring</u> is published and becomes a bestseller. "Over increasingly large areas of the United States, spring now comes unheralded by the return of the birds, and the early mornings are strangely silent where once they were filled with the beauty of birdsong," she writes. "We spray our elms and the following springs are silent of robin song, not because we sprayed the robins directly but because the poison traveled, step by step, through the now familiar elm-leaf-earthworm cycle. These are matters of record, observable, part of the visible world around us. They reflect the web of life-or death- that scientists know as ecology." The insecticide industry fights back, fiercely criticizing the book and its author.

- 1963: Spurred by <u>Silent Spring</u>, the Clean Air Act passes. Only 487 nesting pairs of bald eagles remain in the lower 48 states of the US.

- 1964: Rachel Carson dies. If she had lived longer, would she have written a book about climate change? "We live in an age of rising seas," she had written. "In our own lifetime we are witnessing a startling alteration of climate."

- 1964 and 1965: Congress passes the Wilderness Act and the Water Quality Act, both influenced by <u>Silent Spring</u>.

- 1967: The first list of endangered species is created. It includes bald eagles.

- 1970: The first Earth Day is celebrated on April 22.

- 1970: The Environmental Protection Agency (EPA) is founded.

- 1972: The Clean Water Act passes, and DDT is banned in the US.

- 1980: Rachel Carson is honored posthumously (after death) with the Presidential Medal of Freedom.

- 2007: The bald eagle is removed from the federal list of threatened and endangered species.

Facts About Malaria

(according to the World Health Organization)

- Almost half of the world's population is at risk for malaria.
- 92% of malaria deaths are in Africa.
- 70% of malaria deaths are children under the edge of 5.
- Prevention is key, but an early diagnosis and treatment makes a big difference in outcome.

  - Only certain mosquitoes (species of the genus Anopheles) are vectors for malaria, and only female mosquitoes carry it. The mosquitoes become vectors when they bite someone who has malaria, which they transmit when they bite someone else. The fewer people have malaria, the fewer people will get it.

My Ideas

- Earth Day and World Malaria Day are in the same week of April. How can we combine these to help locally and globally?
- Try to get businesses to sponsor an Earth Day trash cleanup. Will they agree to donate a dollar to malaria research for every pound of litter that we pick up near their place of business?
- Have a community yard sale and use all the proceeds to buy mosquito nets, for kids to sleep under at night in parts of the world where malaria is prevalent.

DDT

NEW SCIENCE WORDS

Biomagnification

The growing concentration of a toxin as it goes up a food chain. Animals higher in the food chain accumulate higher levels of the toxin.

Food Web

A system of interconnecting food chains.

Insecticide

A substance that controls or kill insects that people consider harmful.

Pesticide

A substance that controls or kills organisms that people think are harmful. A pesticide that targets insects is called an insecticide. A pesticide that targets plants is called an herbicide.

Food Chain

Plants on land and phytoplankton and algae in the sea are primary producers, making organic matter from carbon dioxide, nutrients, and the sun's energy. Animals that eat plants are herbivores. Animals that eat other animals are carnivores. Animals that eat plants and animals are omnivores. Each sequence of a plant, the animal that eats it, the animal that eats that animal, and so on is a food chain. At the top of the chain is an apex predator (like a lion or a killer whale) that nothing else in the local environment is able to prey on.

Grasshopper

Frog

Food Chain

Grass

Snake

Raptor

A mosquito gorging on human blood. Yuck!

Malaria

A disease caused by a microscopic parasite that is carried by mosquitoes in tropical regions of the planet. A mosquito bite can transmit the parasite into a human host's blood, where it matures and multiplies. Without treatment, malaria can be deadly.

Things I Still Wonder:

- If bacteria can build up a resistance to antibiotics, can insects build up a resistance to insecticides?

- I get vaccines for the flu and chickenpox. Are there vaccines for malaria and Lyme disease?

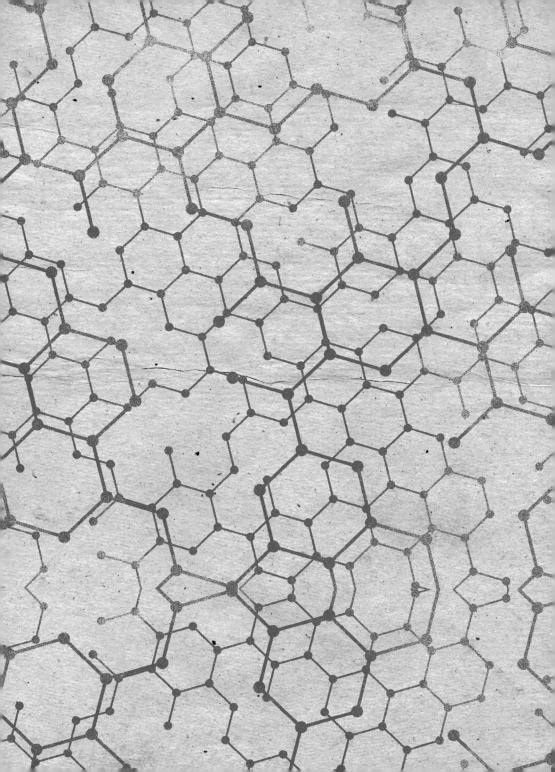

5
A Year of Science

It's a beautiful spring day. The sun is shining, the breeze is warm, and flowers are in bloom. Acadia breathes in the sweet smell of lilacs and kicks the soccer ball to Joshua. Joshua shoots the ball toward the corner of the goal, but Isabel blocks it.

"Nice block!" Joshua says, as Isabel rolls the ball back to him.

Acadia looks over her shoulder at her mom, who is carrying trays of seedlings toward the garden. "You two keep playing. I'll be right back," she says, and runs over to her mom, who is looking thoughtfully at the garden before deciding where to set down a tray.

"What're you doing, Mom?"

"I'm trying to plan the garden."

"Why do you look stressed?"

"I'm not stressed. It's just tricky. Some plants need more sun than others, and others need more space to grow."

"When you don't know what to do, you should . . . ." Acadia raises an eyebrow.

Acadia's mom looks confused. "Ask someone?"

"Well, you could ask someone, or you could make it into . . . ." Acadia gives her mom another significant look.

"A game?"

"No, make it into an experiment. Research the vegetables, then try them out and keep track of what grows well where. Then you'll know for sure for next year."

"You sound like the science teacher now."

"You can even come up with a hypothesis."

"Like you did for your blueberries?"

"Yep. My hypothesis was right. The blueberry thieves were birds. But I also learned that the soccer net's holes were too big. This year I'm going to try mesh nets with small holes, and if that doesn't work, I'll do more research and come up with something else."

Acadia mom smiles. "Spoken like a true scientist."

"I do feel kind of like a scientist. I've filled most of a notebook with everything I've learned over the past year."

"Acadia, come play!" Joshua yells as he kicks the soccer ball to her.

"Gotta go, Mom. Good luck with the garden!"

When Acadia kicks the ball, it rolls toward Baxter, who is lying in the shade. Acadia looks up at the bright sun and knows why it feels so strong. It's almost summer, and the northern half of Earth will soon be tilted at its most direct angle toward the sun. She understands that while it's about to be summer here, it's about to be winter in the southern hemisphere. When it's warm here, it's cold there. When it's cold here, it's warm there. Everything on Earth has a balance—even the seasons.

A bird flies by, and Baxter leaps up and runs after it. But, like always, the bird is faster than he is. Acadia thinks about the many ways that species survive—from the tiny tick that clings to its host to the maple tree in her yard that loses its leaves in the fall. Everything in nature is just trying to survive. She thinks about Joshua, who was trying to survive too when he used to make mean comments, and how much he has changed in the past year.

Joshua kicks the ball toward Acadia's dad, who is taking down laundry from the clothesline. Joshua points to the clothesline and says, "I like your new solar-powered dryer."

Acadia's dad smiles at his joke. "Good one. Yes, we're working on reducing our carbon footprint."

Acadia walks over to the two of them. "We're having *loads* of fun with it, right Dad?" Acadia tries to keep a straight face but can't stifle a little laugh. "I'm sorry, that was terrible laundry humor."

Acadia's dad puts his arm around her and says, "That's my girl."

Isabel walks over to the group. "What should we do now?"

"It's so beautiful," Acadia says, grabbing a towel off the clothesline. "I kind of want to lie on the grass and look up at the clouds."

"Sounds good to me," Isabel says.

"Me too," Joshua seconds.

As they lie next to each other, Isabel says, "I love doing nothing. Soon we can be doing this at the beach. Just think of the sandcastles we'll build and all the swimming we'll do."

Baxter runs over and curls up beside them. Acadia rests her hand on his warm back, breathes in the fresh air, and looks up at the fluffy clouds. As their shapes change, she wonders why the clouds look like puffy cotton balls today, while on other days they look like ripples across the sky. She thinks about the weather and wonders why it changes, and if the forces that change the weather also change the clouds.

Acadia hears a "Chickadee-dee-dee, chickadee-dee-dee" echo through the warm spring air and sits up in time to see a bird fly toward her blueberry bushes. She can't help but smile at how much she has learned and how many additional questions her newfound knowledge leads to. Looking at the world around her, she feels excited for all the learning that is yet to come.

That night, Acadia flips through her science notebook and sees how much she has learned over the past year. She also realizes that much of what she now understands is interconnected.

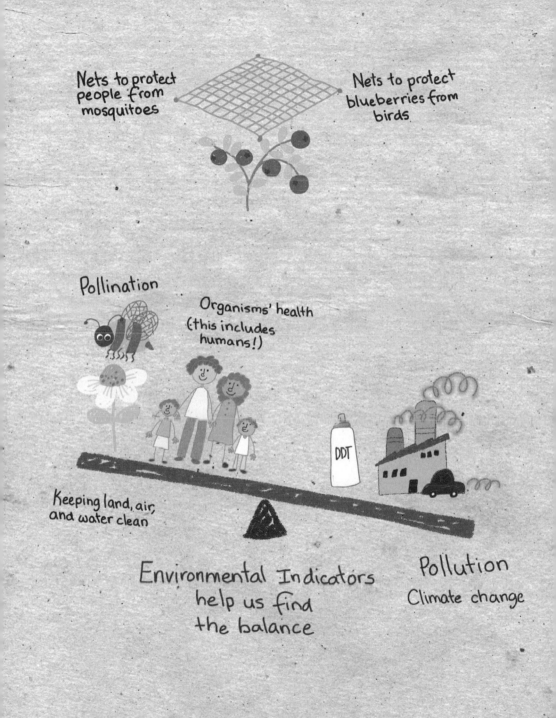

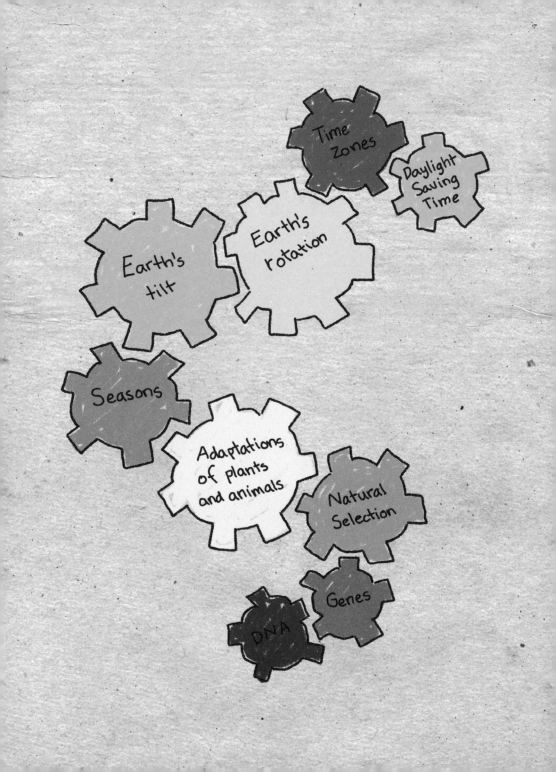

Tides

Paper airplanes ← **Force** → Erosion

Impact of meteors

sledding

Malaria

Lyme Disease

Allergies

Immune System

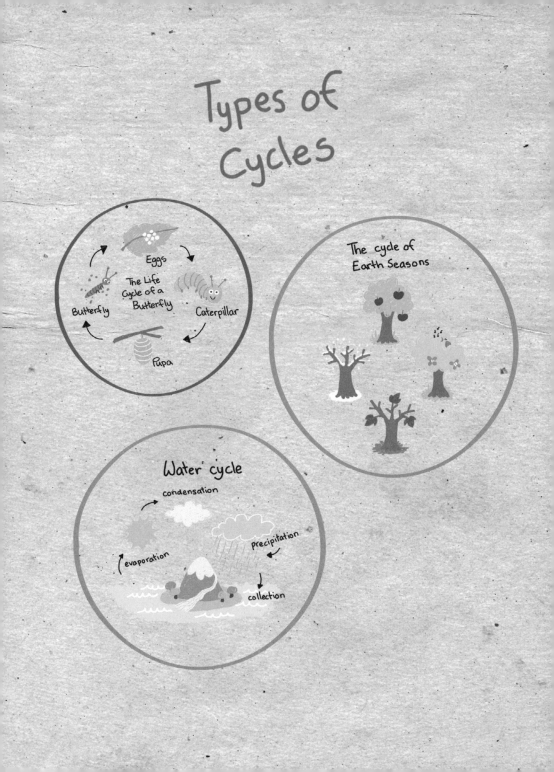

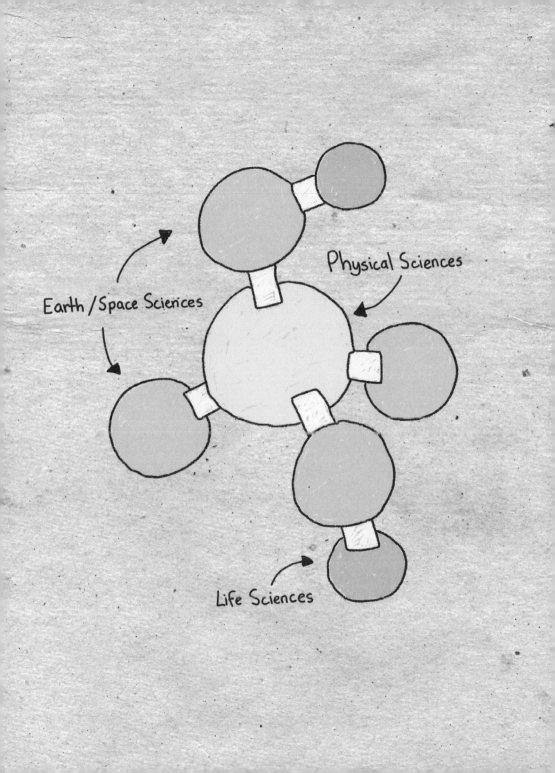

Earth / Space Sciences

Physical Sciences

Life Sciences

NEW SCIENCE WORDS

These are all the <u>New Science Words</u> I learned in the past year!

Summer

Scientific Method
Hypothesis
Evidence
Conclusion
Genetics
Genes
DNA
Dominant Traits
Recessive Traits
Weathering
Sediment
Erosion
Deposition
Revolution
Elliptical
Rotation
Axis
Gravity
Gravitational Pull
Force

Autumn

Environmental Indicator
Abiotic Factors
Biotic Factors
Organism
Cells
Photosynthesis
Chlorophyll
Producer
Consumer
Water Cycle
Transpiration
Evaporation
Condensation
Precipitation
Time Zone
International Date Line
Greenwich Mean Time
Standard Time
White Blood Cells
Bone Marrow
Lymph Nodes
Spleen
Skin

Winter

Climate
Climate Change
Atmosphere
Carbon Footprint
Fossil Fuels
Global Warming
Greenhouse Effect
Element
Atom
Molecule
Aerodynamic
Drag
Lift
Thrust
Adaptation
Hibernation
Migration
Natural Selection
Force
Friction
Acceleration
Potential Energy
Kinetic Energy

Spring

Asteroid
Meteor
Meteorite
Crater
Momentum
Pollen
Germination
Hatching
Life Cycle
Parasite
Host
Arachnids
Vector
Pesticide
Food Chain
Food Web
Biomagnification
Malaria

Things I Still Wonder:

- What will I learn next?

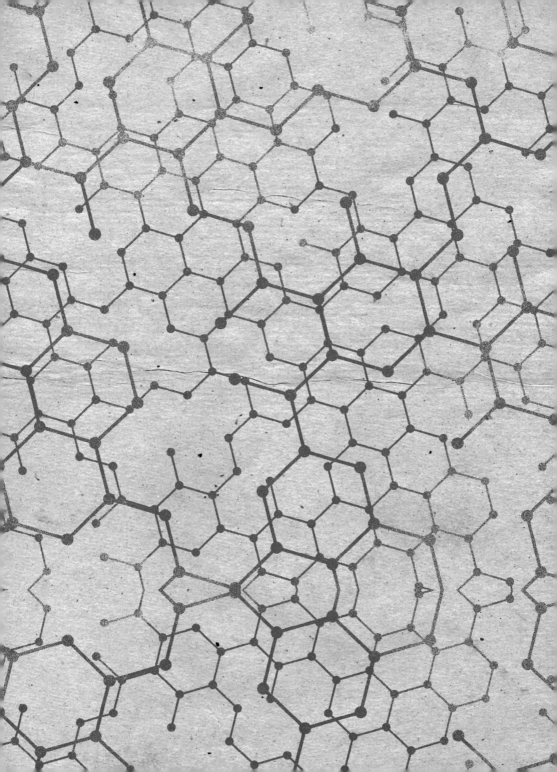

Further Exploration

The following websites were helpful to me while writing this book and are likely to remain active and helpful to teachers and learners in the years to come.

Catch a Falling Star (Chapter 1)

Meteors

https://spaceplace.nasa.gov/craters/en/

https://www.esa.int/esaKIDSen/Cometsandmeteors.html

Space

https://solarsystem.nasa.gov/planets/earth/overview/

https://www.nasa.gov/kidsclub/index.html

https://www.esa.int/esaKIDSen/SEMT0EBE8JG_LifeinSpace_0.html

Mass Extinctions

https://www.amnh.org/exhibitions/dinosaurs-ancient-fossils-new-discoveries/extinction/mass-extinction/

https://evolution.berkeley.edu/evolibrary/article/0_0_0/massextinct_01

KT Extinction

http://www.pbs.org/wgbh/evolution/extinction/dinosaurs/asteroid.html

http://www.chicxulubcrater.org/

https://www.sciencenewsforstudents.org/article/dinosaurs-extinction-asteroid-eruptions-doom

Signs of the Season (Chapter 2)

Signs of Spring

https://www.woodlandtrust.org.uk/naturedetectives/activities/2016/01/first-signs-of-spring/

https://www.nature.org/ourinitiatives/regions/northamerica/unitedstates/5-signs-of-spring.xml

https://www.learner.org/jnorth/spring/

Pollination

https://www.fs.fed.us/wildflowers/pollinators/What_is_Pollination/

http://pollinator.org/pollination

https://treesforlife.org.uk/forest/forest-ecology/pollination/

Bees

https://www.npr.org/sections/thetwo-way/2017/01/11/509337678/u-s-puts-first-bumblebee-on-the-endangered-species-list

https://www.acsh.org/news/2018/01/29/honey-bees-have-gone-endangered-dangerous-and-science-journalism-problem-12488

https://climatekids.nasa.gov/bees/

About Ticks (Chapter 3)

Parasites

https://www.cdc.gov/parasites/index.html

https://medlineplus.gov/parasiticdiseases.html

Ticks

https://www.cdc.gov/ticks/index.html

https://kidshealth.org/en/parents/tick-bites-sheet.html

https://extension.umaine.edu/ipm/tickid/maine-tick-species/

Lyme Disease

https://childrensnational.org/choose-childrens/conditions-and-treatments/infectious-diseases/lyme-disease

https://www.maine.gov/dhhs/mecdc/infectious-disease/epi/vector-borne/lyme/

Earth Day, DDT, and Rachel Carson (Chapter 4)

Rachel Carson

http://www.rachelcarson.org/

https://www.womenshistory.org/education-resources/biographies/rachel-carson

https://www.newyorker.com/magazine/2018/03/26/the-right-way-to-remember-rachel-carson

Silent Spring

https://www.nrdc.org/stories/story-silent-spring

https://www.acs.org/content/acs/en/education/whatischemistry/land-marks/rachel-carson-silent-spring.html

http://www.environmentandsociety.org/exhibitions/silent-spring/leg-acy-rachel-carsons-silent-spring

DDT

http://www.panna.org/resources/ddt-story

http://pmep.cce.cornell.edu/profiles/extoxnet/carbaryl-dicrotophos/ddt-ext.html

https://www.epa.gov/ingredients-used-pesticide-products/ddt-brief-history-and-status

Malaria

https://www.cdc.gov/parasites/malaria/index.html

http://www.who.int/news-room/fact-sheets/detail/malaria

http://www.who.int/malaria/data/en/

Acknowledgments

A huge thank you to Jonathan Eaton and the staff at Tilbury House Publishers for believing in this project. Thank you to Holly Hatam and Ana Ochoa for capturing Acadia's journal with their beautiful illustrations.

My husband, Andrew, can be seen throughout these stories by those who know him. He gave feedback and ideas from the first draft through the final revisions. Thank you for the support you show me and the support you always give our family.

Thank you to my grown-up beta readers Andrew McCullough, Lindsay Coppens, and Peggy Becksvoort. Each of you brought a unique lens that made the book better. Thank you to my kid beta readers Greta Holmes, Sylvia Holmes, Isabel Carr, Allison Smart, and Greta Niemann for your honest (and very fun to read!) feedback. And thank you to my students at Falmouth Middle School; the sorts of questions you ask were with me as I wrote the stories and created a vision for Acadia's notebook.

And last but certainly not least, thank you to my fact checkers who helped edit and review the accuracy of the scientific content: Andrew McCullough, Grant Tremblay, Elise Tremblay, Sarah Dawson, Eli Wilson, Jean Barbour, and Bernd Heinrich, who generously answered a question no one else could. A lot of minds and a lot of knowledge are behind this book. I couldn't have done it without them.

KATIE COPPENS lives in Maine with her husband and two children. She is an award-winning middle school language arts and science teacher. Much inspiration from this book came from her marriage to a high school biology teacher and from their focus on raising children instilled with compassion, curiosity, and creativity. Katie's publications include a teacher's guide for the National Science Teachers Association, *Creative Writing in Science: Activities That Inspire*. She welcomes you to visit her at *www.katiecoppens.com*.

Children's book illustrator and graphic designer HOLLY HATAM (Whitby, Ontario) loves to combine line drawings, photography, and texture to create illustrations that pack energy and personality. Her picture books include *What Matters* (SONWA children's awards honorable mention), *Dear Girl*, *Tree Song* and the picture book series *Maxine the Maker*.

ANA OCHOA lives in Mexico and has illustrated children's books including *Miss Pinkeltink's Purse* (Tilbury House, 2018).